Elizabeth Enler

Ransomed

Elizabeth Ender

Illustrated by Louie Roybal III

Published by Ready Writer Press

Cover Design by Jessica Greyson
safiredesigns.blogspot.com

Cover art and illustrations by Louie Roybal III
www.louieroybal.com

Author picture by Jeff Dunn
www.jdunnphotography.com

This is an allegory. Any similarity to spiritual truths is intentional, to historical persons or events other than Jesus Christ and His death and resurrection, coincidental.

All verses are from the King James Version.

ISBN: 0988461498
ISBN-13: 978-0-9884614-9-9

Dedicated to the One who died for me.
I am His.

ACKNOWLEDGMENTS

Thank you to all the girls, older and younger, who asked me to publish this book.
Your comments and suggestions helped me so very much—without
your encouragement it would not have happened!

Thank you especially to my mom, for making it possible for me to write *Ransomed* in
the first place, and for coming back from lunch with your friends with its title!
You are amazing, and the best mom I could ever imagine.

And thank you to my heart-sister for encouraging me as a Christian, inspiring
me as a writer, and being the incredible friend that you are. Your reaction
to this story's first draft started something beautiful.

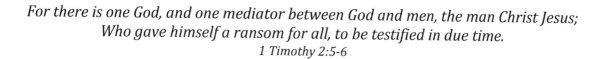

For there is one God, and one mediator between God and men, the man Christ Jesus;
Who gave himself a ransom for all, to be testified in due time.
1 Timothy 2:5-6

"Do not fear for us, my daughter. We will overcome." My lord's quiet words sent strength coursing through my trembling limbs. He reached out his hand, raising me from where I knelt at his feet.

"Look at me."

I lifted my head, seeing in his eyes the love that had sheltered me, fed me, and cared for me since the death of my parents and my betrothal to his son. Every one of the seven years that had passed made me more like his daughter.

"I want you here, safe. Do you understand me?"

I nodded silently. Through the open window of my room, the cries of fighting men and the clash of their weapons echoed inside me, telling me from what he wished to protect me. It also reminded me what I feared for him.

And for his son. My gaze swung instinctively to him, seeking the reassurance I needed.

Immediately my lord's son stepped forward from his place beside his father, his hair

falling across his forehead as it always did when he removed his helmet. His eyes were gentle, and perhaps it was only from the sunlight sparkling off his armor, but I felt tears start to my own eyes at his instant response to my silent plea.

"I've brought you something," he said, his quiet voice pushing back my fears as it always did. In his hand he held a small horn, the beauty of its smoothly polished ivory accentuated by the ornate carvings that decorated it. His initials were worked in among the elaborate scrollwork, and I touched the horn with tentative fingers, glancing up to meet his gaze as he gently placed its thin golden chain around my neck.

"If anything happens . . . if you call me, I will come." His eyes held mine, promising me his help and protection.

His father's voice, suddenly stern, broke into my thoughts. "We must go now—we are needed at the tower. Do not leave this room, or you *will* die."

My eyes widened at his tone. Never before had he spoken to me so sternly. But they were already turning to go. At the door my lord's son looked back, a smile lighting his face.

"We will overcome."

I tried to smile in return, but my fears came rushing back as the door shut behind him. Never before had the enemy gathered such a force. Never before had he dared attack the gates of my lord's castle.

As the sound of their footsteps died away, I began to pace. The noise of the battle rang in my ears, and at last I went to the window and slammed it shut. Why had my lord not vanquished the enemy when his force was small and weak, before he was strong enough to attempt this? I shuddered. If the enemy took the tower, none would be left alive.

I brushed away the tears that were starting to my eyes, attempting to keep them from falling on to the silken dress I wore. My fingers touched the smooth ivory fabric, and the tears would not be held back. It was a gift from my lord. I glanced around the room. Everything in it, all beautiful, all costly, all perfect for my needs, was a gift. He treated me like a daughter, though I was not of his blood and scarce worthy of his favor. And his son—I could not begin to describe how wonderful his son was. They were both so good to me. I closed my eyes, my fingers touching the horn that hung about my neck. He had promised to return.

There was a sudden crash at my window, and my eyes flew open, my hand going to my mouth even as I whirled around to see what had happened. A ladder leaned against my now broken window, and there before me stood a tall stranger, carelessly brushing glass from the black cloak he wore.

Immediately my hand went to the horn. My lord's men wore white and scarlet, and they would never dare to enter my rooms uninvited.

In two quick strides he was at my side, his hand closing over the horn and pulling it from my frightened grasp.

"Will you not give me a chance to explain?"

"Leave my rooms," I breathed, terrified at his nearness. Who *was* he?

"Not unless you come with me. I have come to rescue you."

I tried to wrench the horn from his grasp, but he shook his head.

"Don't go blowing that worthless thing." His fingers tightened on the horn as though he would crush it in his hand, but then he released it, dropping it back against my neck with unutterable scorn.

"He told you he'd come, didn't he? Oh, I've heard that lie before—and seen the horror that awaits the ones who believed it. Go ahead. Blow it. Bring the enemy down upon you, and wait for the rescue that will never come."

His voice was bitter. "Believe me, you will rue the day you listened to his words."

My fingers reached up, touching the horn. Surely it would call him, and he would come. I knew my lord kept his promises; so would his son.

I lifted the horn—but heard my voice instead asking, "What do you mean, 'ones who believed it'?"

He raised his eyebrows. "You don't know? Surely you've wondered where it is he goes when he leaves this castle for weeks at a time. You cannot have thought you were the only girl to whom your beloved lord's son has made promises? To whom he offered one of those?"

He flicked his fingers toward the gift that had just been given me, mocking disbelief in his dark eyes.

Confused, I did not answer. I *had* thought that of my betrothed . . . and this man made it sound so ridiculous that I did. Surely he was lying. Was there any truth in his words? No, there was not.

Where had my lord's son gone when he left? Where had he been, in the days before this attack?

Suddenly the stranger was close to me again, pleading with me, his voice softly gentle.

"Come. Come with me. I will take you to safety—here is danger."

I stepped back away from him, only to find myself clinging desperately to his arm as an explosion shook the floor. In dismay I watched the beautiful glass figurines my lord's son had given me upon his return slide from their place on my table to smash upon the stone floor.

"Look around you," the man whispered in my ear. "You're running out of time."

I let go of his arm. "But—but my lord said to stay here. He commanded me not to leave my rooms! I cannot disobey him."

He looked at me with disbelief written across his face. "Little lady—did he truly order you to stay here, in this room, with a battle raging just outside your door?"

I nodded, confused by the anger suddenly in his eyes. "He—he said I was to stay here, else I would die."

"Really." His eyes narrowed. "So not only does he not care about the danger to which he is exposing you, he threatens you on top of that, merely to force your obedience to his foolish command."

My mouth dropped open. He had not been threatening me! Yet—I had thought my lord's parting words severe. *Had* it been a threat?

The sounds of another explosion rang in my ears, and again the floor shook, though not so much as before. The stranger darted to the window, and I covered my ears, trying to shut out the sound of someone screaming in agony, the voice rising above the noise of battle.

The man turned back from the window, the look on his face commanding my attention. "You must come with me if you want to live. The enemy has taken the tower—"

At that I cried out. Surely the enemy could not have won! He could not have!

"Oh, do not worry. Your precious lord and his son were safe before I even got here. They slipped away when it grew dangerous; you can trust them for that. And if they were coming for you, they would have been here by now. Believe me, little lady. You must!"

"But he said—"

"You will not die if you leave—you will die if you do not! Hurry, we must away. I want to save your life. Hark!" He flung up his hand, and I heard the cheering of victorious men rising up from the ring of battle.

"Come with me," he said softly.

And I went.

The ride was long, and I quickly grew weary of the swift pace, but he was determined that we not be overtaken by the enemy, and he pushed on even as it grew dark. I rode behind him on his horse, trying to ignore the jarring of the beast's rough gait.

Yet the miles did not seem as long as they might have, for he kept my mind from dwelling on the length of our flight with stories of the country through which we rode. The things he spoke of I had never before heard, and at the first tale I pulled away from my rescuer, telling him that my lord had never done the things he was saying—and it was certainly not my lord's fault that the countryside looked the way it did. *He* had not started the fighting that was devastating the land.

He turned slightly in the saddle to look at me. "And how would you know? Has he not kept you sheltered, secluded, away from those who would tell you the truth of the one who guards you? How could you possibly know the depths of his desire for power, or the lengths to which he is willing to go to fulfill that desire?"

To that I had no answer, except the goodness my lord had always shown me. He would never willingly cause the bloodshed that had occurred. At my reply the man laughed.

"You do not even know what it is he has kept from you. You think him good, merely because you have known nothing else. Yet how many times has he forbidden something you wanted? How many times has he refused you what you asked?"

Suddenly I realized the hurt that still lingered inside me from my lord's refusal to allow me to accompany his son the last time he had gone . . . wherever it was he went. I shut my mouth without replying.

Shaking his head, the man faced forward again, saying softly, "And you blindly trust him still!"

He sighed. "What I would not give to have such a trust. Such a faith in me . . . and truly, little lady, I would not disappoint. Look!"

He waved his hands toward the fields through which we rode. We were now beyond my lord's borders, and farther than I had ever before gone. Men and women were everywhere, walking slowly toward their homes in the gathering dusk. I had never seen so many people in one place, and I said so.

With a smile he looked back at me. "There are more people on the grounds of my castle than your wonderful lord has in all his far-reaching lands. Do you notice anything else?"

I glanced around. It was silent; there was no singing as I had often heard around the castle of my lord, but then, it was very late in the day and they were doubtless tired. It was strange they were just now finishing work, I thought, before gasping in surprise as something else caught my attention.

Now I knew what he had wanted me to notice. Each one of them, the most common laborer and the lowest slave, wore a single black jewel somewhere on their persons. I had never seen such jewels as those, so large, so fine, glittering in the last light of the evening sun, promising to glisten even more beautifully by the light of day.

"Oh, how did they get them?"

He laughed. "I give them away. To anyone who wants one. Would you like one? Ah, but I should not ask. Of course you do. And besides, you have already earned one, by coming with me, by renouncing your precious lord."

I opened my mouth to disagree, but then shut it. By disobeying my lord, had I not given my allegiance to the one who even now was carrying me away? I did not want to think of what my lord would say to what I had done—or what he would do. Several tales of his cruelty were even now spinning in my head, and as the horse we rode slowed to a stop before the dark bulk of a castle, black against a blacker night sky, I pushed away all thoughts of him.

"Thank you, my lord," I murmured as the man helped me down. He looked at me, setting me upon the ground.

"Oh, no. Do not call me lord. Here we have no orders, no overbearing lords and subservient underlings. I am merely a friend who wished to help you."

He led me to the door, holding it open so that I could pass through. Inside it was dark, and I glanced around, striving in vain to see through the blackness ahead. The door swung shut, the moonlight behind me disappearing. Our footsteps echoed as I followed him down the passageway. Suddenly the echoes widened, and I knew we had reached a main entry. Just ahead, a single candle burned upon a table in the center of the room, its small flame unable to dispel the shadows that surrounded us.

He moved away from me, but in a moment he returned. Hanging from his fingers was a pendant, its large black stone catching the light from the candle and seeming to swallow it.

"Here you are, little lady. Allow me." He undid the chain, moving behind me to fasten it around my neck. I pulled my hair over my shoulder out of his way, scarce noticing how the chain of the horn that still hung from my neck seemed to burn as the second chain brushed my skin, sliding up around my throat.

The touch of his cold fingers against my neck sent a chill through me, and when I heard the click of the clasp, I shivered. But the next instant he was before me again, smiling.

"Now you are truly one of us. Let us rejoice!"

I looked down, touching the black jewel that now hung around my neck. It was heavier than I had expected, but surely none could deny its beauty. I raised my head, meeting his gaze with a smile of my own. Truly, there was something delightful in this. To be here, where there were no lords and no underlings, only equals.

Yet when I met his eyes, the chill I had felt from his fingers swept over me, freezing me with a dreadful coldness.

Even before my eyes he grew taller, the blackness that surrounded us seeming to enter into him. Or perhaps it all came from him to start with; I could not tell.

The single candle flickered suddenly, going out with a faint sizzle.

His soft laugh was mocking, evil, terrifying in the darkness.

"Or perhaps I should say . . . *now you are mine.*"

I trembled, and I could not keep my voice from shaking.

"What do you mean?"

His hands were suddenly on my shoulders, and he was shaking me so hard my head snapped back, even as I gasped in pain at the tightness of his grasp.

"Call me master when you speak, for so I am. We have no lords here, truly—your lord is far away, and you have left him. But I am your master, and you are my *slave.*"

At last I found my voice. "Let go of me!" I whispered, attempting to jerk away from him.

Again he laughed, and I felt my strength leave me at the sound.

"You do not yet understand. Perhaps a night here will help."

He stepped forward, pulling me along, and I heard the sound of a door opening. A sudden rush of cold air, ancient smelling and wet, blew by me. Before I had time to think, he shoved me forward, and I screamed even as I felt myself falling, falling into darkness.

I landed on stone, the breath knocked from me and pain shooting up the hands that had been outstretched in my fall. There I lay, dizzy and hurt, gasping for breath, while his laughter drifted down to me from above. Distantly I heard his voice, pleasure filling it.

"The battle today was not a complete loss, at least. Good night, little lady. Sleep well!"

The slam of a door followed his words, and then the thud of a bolt being shoved into place.

I shuddered, beginning to sob as I caught my breath. Dampness soaked through my dress, and I sat up slowly, whimpering at the pain in my wrists.

What have I done?

As I sat upright, full realization crashed over me, and I crumpled back down, hiding my face in my arms. How could I have believed him for an instant? He was the enemy, the one who had rebelled against my lord—who had refused my lord's pardon—who had attacked my lord's castle—*who was now my master.*

Again I shuddered, horror filling me as I realized the truth of those words and thought of what lay before me. I had entered the castle of my lord's enemy . . . the enemy whose cruelty was known far and wide across the land, and whose hatred for my lord and all he held dear was second only to his desire for power.

He was right in one thing—I *had* been sheltered, protected from his vicious brutality. Now, dark rumors, whispered even in broad daylight, returned to haunt me, and I could feel fear closing in about me. I had willingly put myself in his power, and there was no end to his malice.

Something rustled in the dark, tiny feet scampering across the wet floor. I rose, trembling in the darkness, my fingers fumbling for the horn around my neck.

Instead they touched the black stone, and in anger I jerked it violently, attempting to break the thin chain from which it hung. The chain bit into my neck but held tight, merely bruising my skin. I felt for the clasp, but it would not open. Then I closed my eyes in the darkness, understanding at last the mark of slavery that I wore.

Dropping my hands in defeat, I again thought of the horn.

My hand reached up, fingers gently brushing its surface. I clasped it against me, picturing the one who had given it to me. I thought I had loved him ever since I had first seen him. Yet somehow that had not been enough to keep me with him, safe in the castle of his father.

At that thought I caught my breath, the realization of all I had lost suddenly overwhelming me. He had said he would come for me, but to hold to the betrothal after I had run from him, straight to the worst enemy of his father and himself? I clutched the horn more tightly between my fingers.

I wanted to blow it, to call him to my rescue. But even as I wanted it, I blushed at the thought of seeing him again. How foolish I had been! How ungrateful! And I had outright disobeyed my lord.

Yet there was also fear in me. Surely the horn would have been taken from me if it had any power to bring me rescue? Was not its very presence about my neck merely another way to mock me?

I clutched the horn more tightly. He had promised . . . Oh, but if he did not come! That I could not bear.

Bowing my head, I began to weep. I had believed the lies of the enemy rather than obey the one who had so lovingly cared for me. I was a traitor to my lord and unfaithful to my beloved. Loathing was not a strong enough word for what I felt for myself at that instant. I wanted to die.

Then I realized how probable it was that I soon would.

Yet I did not. Now I understood my lord's words, and the living death I now endured was so much worse than the quick death I had feared while safe in his castle—that death I now longed for. But no matter how I wished for death, it did not come, and I could not obtain it. The chain about my neck kept even that from me.

The first morning dawned clear, the brilliance of the blue sky and the cheerfulness of the bright sun mocking the despair that filled the place in which I found myself. There was no end to the fields that needed tending, and I was taken from the dungeon and immediately set to digging one of the many water ditches that irrigated the sandy soil.

I had seen those who worked the lands about the castle of my lord and thought their labor hard, for I myself had never done such work. But I had never imagined work like this, agonizing drudgery unlightened by any thought of future joy or reward.

When I looked around, there was nothing but sullen misery on the faces of the other slaves. No one spoke; they scarce seemed to notice each other. From the looks of them, they never ate the food they were so painstakingly cultivating, and I realized that my lack of a morning meal was probably customary. These fields grew food for the army . . . the army that fought against my lord and his son.

My beautiful clothing was utterly impractical, and I kept tripping on the hem of my skirt, but soon I did not care. The sun grew hotter, and blisters quickly formed on my palms, while my muscles burned with the effort of lifting out the sand. By the time the sun was straight overhead, I thought I could not possibly raise another shovelful. Panting, I leaned against the handle of the shovel, moving my blistered hands away from the splintery wood.

Suddenly the section of the ditch I had been working upon gave way, and sand poured back down into the space I had so laboriously emptied. I wanted to cry.

There was a sudden shout behind me, and those slaves nearest me stepped quickly away. I turned to see an overseer bearing down upon me, his face furious, a many-tailed whip clenched in his fist.

That day and the scars I earned were only the beginning, and I soon found that, in this land, there was no hope that the future would be better. Rather, everything only grew worse.

The others and I worked or we were punished; often, we worked and were punished anyway. At any hour of the day, screams could be heard as some slave received a whipping, or a worse penalty, for failing to do exactly what he had been ordered to do. Yet it was not even a shared suffering. The others hated me as I hated myself, and would never have dreamed of helping me, any more than I could imagine trying to help them. I had never felt so alone.

Some seemed to grow stronger through the pain, but I grew only weaker. The days passed in slow torment, and at night I would collapse against the hard pallets of the huts in which we slept, surprised to find myself still living, still breathing.

Yet somehow my life continued on, day after soul-crushing day, until at last, in the heat of midday, as the sun beat down upon us, the man beside me crumpled to the ground, simply unable to go on. The overseer was upon him in a moment, the heavy lash of the whip falling over and over in hideous repetition. I found myself backing away with the others, but when they halted, I kept backing. Escape was utterly impossible, yet in that moment I turned and ran. Surely nothing could be worse than the existence I was now enduring.

Or so I thought until I was dragged before my master, having scarcely passed the boundaries that had been set for us. He smiled slightly, but did not speak to me, ordering only that I be taken to the great hall.

This time slaves gathered close, eager to know of another who was worse off than they themselves, and knowing that I alone would bear the punishment for attempting to escape. Those who held me threw me down upon the smooth rock floor at his feet, where I swayed on my knees, waiting in shuddering silence to learn my fate. My master too was silent, and every minute seemed an age as I waited.

"So ungrateful . . ." he said at last, his fingers tapping a beat against the polished wood of the chair's arm as he decided my fate. The voice that haunted my dreams was now so soft, yet not hiding the underlying threat in the least. "What is it we do to those who dare show such ingratitude?"

I shuddered beneath his gaze, and then he rose, speaking forcefully that all might hear.

"When one attempts to leave my service, there can but one thing follow. At daybreak

tomorrow you will be chained in the center of the castle courtyard and executed by slow fire."

The words slammed into me, making the room spin about me. As if from a great distance I could hear his footsteps as he came down the steps of the raised dais, and I felt the air swirling as he passed close beside me, but I could neither move nor speak.

Then I was hauled to my feet, taken to a small room, and chained to keep me until the morrow. The others departed quickly, leaving me to face the long hours of the night, and what would come after them, alone. Each moment that stretched slowly by left me less prepared to endure.

At last I thought of the horn. It had entered my mind less and less of late . . . yet if I did not try it now, I would never have another chance. I lifted one hand, my fingers brushing against the horn, but at the thought of seeing my betrothed in such a state and in such a place, after what I had done, I jerked my hand away. Yet I knew what it truly was that stayed my will. If I blew it and nothing happened—that thought frightened me more than anything. So long as I did not ask for help, I could hope. I could yet believe in his promises and his love.

If he did not come, what did I have left? There was nothing then, nothing in the world at all but lies and evil. The one I betrayed had lied to me, and the one whom I had followed decreed my death. No, I would rather believe there had indeed been truth in the eyes of the one who had promised to come for me than call him and know I had been deceived.

Then the morning light filtered in through arrow slits high in the wall, and I knew what it was that lay before me. To die with hope was still to die, and already I could feel the flames licking my flesh.

Then I raised my chained hands, lifting the horn to my lips. Shutting my eyes, I blew the horn, hearing the low, yet strangely sweet sound reverberate from the walls about me.

Almost immediately there were steps outside the door, and the bolt was drawn back. The horn dropped from my shaking hands as I waited for my master to enter and kill me.

The door opened, and I lifted my eyes—as my lord's son entered the room. His sword in his hand, he pushed open the door. Catching sight of me, he stared for a moment, sorrow spreading across his face at the sight of my chains. He stepped nearer, kneeling beside me.

"Why did you not call me sooner? I have been searching for you since you disappeared! I could not find you until you called."

I began to weep, words disappearing in a rush of emotion that threatened to suffocate me. Had I not been chained, I would have thrown myself at his feet. Seeing the love and pity in his eyes, I wept harder. Through my sobs, I heard footsteps approaching. It was my master.

"Go! He will kill you! Leave quickly!" I frantically whispered, finding my voice in a sudden wave of terror.

He looked at me gently and shook his head. "How could I leave you?" he asked, and turned to face my master.

I wanted to hide my face, but I could not. Instead, I watched as the man threw himself at my lord's son with his sword drawn, attempting to end the confrontation immediately. My lord's son knocked the sword away, moving away from me as he did so, that I would not be in danger. My breath caught at this small gesture of his care, and I dashed the tears from my eyes, feeling as if a dagger had gone through my heart. If he died here, I had but poured his

blood upon my hands in my desperate cry for his help, adding murder to betrayal.

Then their swords were ringing as they met and the fight began in earnest. It seemed my master must win, and I think my heart stopped its beating for a moment. Then once more my lord's son was pressing the other back, and I could breath again, until once more he himself was moving backwards, forced into a corner by the man who fought him. I bit my lip until blood flowed to keep from screaming aloud.

Before I quite knew what had happened, their positions were suddenly reversed, and my lord's son had his sword at the other's throat.

"Turn her loose immediately." The command was calm, giving no hint of how his heart must be pounding after such a fight.

The other smiled savagely, joyfully almost. "No! She followed me of her own free will. Now she is mine. You cannot have her."

My lord's son whirled toward me. "You went with him of your own free will?" The question was incredulous.

"Yes," I barely whispered, the truth of those words seeming to overwhelm me with their hopelessness even as I realized his effort might have been entirely in vain. "Is there no way you can save me? I am sorry! Forgive me, please! Just save me—this once!" My voice died away, and I realized I was trembling, the chains upon my wrists seeming to bind me more tightly than ever before.

He looked at me a long moment. Then he turned to my master, regarding him silently. At last he motioned for him to step out of the room with him, and they shut the door as they went out. I could hear murmured voices through the thick stone wall, and I closed my eyes, afraid to know what they were saying.

Finally, they returned. My lord's son looked somehow older, and more tired than he had directly after the sword fight, with a heaviness in his step that I had never before seen. But there was the hint of a smile upon my master's face, nothing of defeat about him in the least, and I felt dizziness fill my mind, knowing he had received his desire.

Yet he came toward me, pulling a large key from inside his cloak, his smile deepening as he looked at me. "He has ransomed you," he said, as if he still could not quite believe it.

My lord's son took the key from him and gently unlocked my shackles. He helped me to my feet, and together we walked to the door of the castle. I stumbled beside him, too confused to understand what was happening though I clung to his hand as to the only thing holding me back from a fiery death.

Two of my lord's horses stood outside, cropping grass near the road. My lord's son motioned for me to mount one of them. He lifted me into the saddle and then smiled sadly at me. Tears were still running down my face.

"Go home, and come here no more." Without warning he smacked the horse I was on sharply. The horse leaped forward into a headlong gallop. Twisting in the saddle, I saw my lord's son going back into the castle.

Then I knew, with sudden shocking clarity that drove the breath from my body. He had traded himself for me.

I clung to the saddle, blinded by pain and tears, seeing him enter that castle over and over in my mind. How could he have done it? I could not believe it. Torment swept over me as I pictured him taking my place.

In sudden anguish I reached for the reins that lay against the horse's neck, pulling him to a stop and attempting to turn him back the way we had come. He shook his head angrily, half-reared, and began to gallop even more swiftly toward his home.

His home. It had once been my home . . . and I was returning to it. Yet there was no joy in the thought, only sickening loss and guilt. I dreaded seeing my lord, but now I knew I could not disobey his son's last words to me.

Again sorrow swept over me. What could I say to my lord? How could I tell him what his son had done? *For me?* My heart ached with pain so sharp it hurt to breathe.

They had surely come to my rooms on that long ago day, ready to rejoice over their victory. I had not been there. And my lord's son had been searching for me, waiting for me to call him, fool that I was ever to doubt his promise and break my own.

After some time, the horse began to slow, unable to keep up the swift pace. Every hour seemed an age, and I scarce noticed as the land changed from overworked barrenness to the green rolling hills that had become a distant memory. On we traveled, now merely at a walk, through the heat of midday. The sun beat down upon us both, its bright rays a vicious reminder of what my betrothed had chosen to endure in my place.

It was late when we neared the castle, yet the gates had not been closed. The horse carried me through them, stopping at last before the keep. I slid from his back, trembling with exhaustion and grief.

The door of the keep opened. There before me stood my lord, the one who had been a father, protector, guide, and friend to me. He was dressed as for a feast, and there was glad welcome upon his face, the look in his eyes going through me more sharply than any sword.

I threw myself at his feet, unable to say a word. Could he tell my heart was breaking? Suddenly I felt his arms around me, and he lifted me up and embraced me—as though I were not a filthy, ragged, rebellious girl who had left him, believing lies about his goodness.

"My daughter," was all he said, and yet I could feel his forgiveness and love.

"Oh, my lord!" I cried, once more beginning to weep. "Your son . . ."

"My son?"

I thought I could not say it, but I heard my strangled voice whispering, "I called him—" The words choked me then, and shadows were swirling through my head.

"He went with my blessing," my lord said gently, "to do whatever was necessary to bring you home."

The darkness took me then, weakness and pain demanding their toll at last. I felt myself collapsing, but I knew he would not let me fall.

It was the last I knew for three days, or so I was told after I awoke. I felt anguish before I opened my eyes, and it was but a moment before I remembered why. The pain that followed was too great to bear with my eyes closed, and I opened them with a gasp, flinching at the sunlight dancing upon the coverlet.

I was in my old room, the hangings about my bed drawn back to allow in the light from the windows, and I turned my face away from the sun with a desperate aching.

Then the world itself seemed to stand still, time frozen into nothingness, for there *he* was, seated beside my bed with a quiet smile upon his face. I could not comprehend it, but it was indeed my lord's son.

Wounded, bruised, bloodied—but alive. I sat up, my hands unconsciously reaching out toward him as tears started unbidden to my eyes.

"How—what?" I gasped, my mind still insisting it could not be.

"By taking your place, as one who had never chosen to follow the enemy—"

I bowed my head in shame but could not drag my eyes from his face.

"—you were freed. By law he could not order my death by fire, and he did not realize I was still lord, even whipped and chained. He had to accept my challenge at last, and afterward I came home."

He smiled at me tenderly.

I dropped my hands and lowered my gaze, unable now to look at him.

"He is defeated. You need not fear."

I turned my face away. I could not say it was not *that* man I feared. My lord's son had come home—but what had I done? What now was to be my fate, a traitor and a rebel who had so very nearly cost him his life? I knew what I deserved, and the mere thought of seeing the pain and condemnation that should be in his eyes nearly overwhelmed me.

Then I felt his arms enfolding me, drawing me close.

"You are safe with me."

His forgiveness surrounded me, covering me like the waves of an ocean, as I lifted my head and stared at him in amazement. I shuddered, seeing the bruises and cuts that covered his face and, I am sure, the rest of him.

"How could you do it for me?" I asked, my voice breaking.

"I would do more for you," he said simply. "You are to be my bride."

I shook my head, blinded by my tears. "After all I have done, how I have behaved to you, how foolish I have been, you would *marry* me? A runaway and a slave?"

He tightened one arm about my shoulders, lifting his other hand to my neck. The chain that held the black stone close against my throat disintegrated at his touch, and the stone fell to the edge of the bed, slipping to the ground without a sound. He smiled gently at me.

"You are mine," he said softly.

A week had not yet passed when I saw my lord's son preparing for a journey.

"Where are you going?" I asked him hesitantly, wondering that he was well enough to travel.

"There are many still in bondage, as you were," he said. "I go to rescue them."

"But my love!" I cried desperately. You may be killed! He who was my master—"

"I have already conquered him, remember?" he said with a smile. "All that remains is to find those entrapped by him and tell them that they may go free." He looked at me. "I am leaving the people of this country to you. Tell them what I have done."

I stared at him. "He had no slaves near your castle, had he?"

He nodded. "His slaves are everywhere—and they need be slaves no longer. I am going to the far corners of this land to find them. Our wedding will be when I return, and you will come with me to my own castle. For now, my father is ready to give you anything you need; simply ask him."

He reached out and touched the horn hanging around my neck. "If you need me, call me, and I will come."

A smile was on his lips and a promise in his eyes, but I shuddered, remembering.

Swinging himself up on to his horse, he looked down at me, and I knew he saw what I was thinking.

"Do not be afraid," he said softly. "Just remember how much I love you."

Again he smiled, and then I watched him ride through the gate, his sword at his side.

Now I must go and do the work my lord's son has given me. Remembering my own slavery makes me long to help those now in unnecessary bondage. Knowing his great love every day makes me long to please him. Soon he will return, and I wish to be ready, for the words he spoke are true.

I am his.

AUTHOR'S NOTE

The girl in this story represents me—and you. God, who is not willing that any should perish, loves us so much that He made a way for us to escape the slavery of sin and live an abundant life with Him. If you know and believe this, I hope *Ransomed* helps you see again the awesomeness of what Christ did for you. If you don't, please find a Bible, email me at elizabeth.c.ender@gmail.com, do whatever you can to learn the truth of His death and resurrection and how it will affect you for eternity. This is my prayer for you:

We also, since the day we heard it, do not cease to pray for you, and to desire that ye might be filled with the knowledge of his will in all wisdom and spiritual understanding; That ye might walk worthy of the Lord unto all pleasing, being fruitful in every good work, and increasing in the knowledge of God; Strengthened with all might, according to his glorious power, unto all patience and longsuffering with joyfulness; Giving thanks unto the Father, which hath made us meet to be partakers of the inheritance of the saints in light: Who hath delivered us from the power of darkness, and hath translated us into the kingdom of his dear Son: In whom we have redemption through his blood, even the forgiveness of sins: Who is the image of the invisible God, the firstborn of every creature: For by him were all things created, that are in heaven, and that are in earth, visible and invisible, whether they be thrones, or dominions, or principalities, or powers: all things were created by him, and for him: And he is before all things, and by him all things consist. And he is the head of the body, the church: who is the beginning, the firstborn from the dead; that in all things he might have the preeminence. For it pleased the Father that in him should all fulness dwell; And, having made peace through the blood of his cross, by him to reconcile all things unto himself; by him, I say, whether they be things in earth, or things in heaven. And you, that were sometime alienated and enemies in your mind by wicked works, yet now hath he reconciled In the body of his flesh through death, to present you holy and unblameable and unreproveable in his sight: if ye continue in the faith grounded and settled, and be not moved away from the hope of the gospel, which ye have heard. ~Colossians 1:9-23

ABOUT THE AUTHOR

Storytelling is in my blood—some of my earliest memories are of listening to my grandparent's stories and of my parents reading to my siblings and me. Even before I knew how to write, I was dictating my own stories for others to write down. Besides being a writer, I am also a home school graduate, private pilot, and medical school student. Above all I am a child of the Most High King, because He loved me, created me, and made me His own through the precious blood of my Savior and Lord, Jesus Christ. The story He is writing is far more incredible than anything we could ever imagine, and by writing my own stories, I hope to glorify Him.

ABOUT THE ILLUSTRATOR

Louie Roybal III attended Pensacola Christian College. He majored in Commercial Art and Graphic Design. He has a love for both, and desires to produce fine art at a casual rate while working in the graphic design industry. Louie currently works full time as a graphic designer, and freelances to selected clients on the side. You can see more of his work at www.louieroybal.com

ABOUT THE BOOK

Visit elizabethender.blogspot.com to learn how purchasing *Ransomed* will benefit an incredible ministry! All net profits from the sale of this book are donated.